CRETA
THE WINGED
TERROR

ST MARY'S
CHURCH OF ENGLAND
PRIMARY SCHOOL

With special thanks to Lucy Courtenay

For Joe Richardson-Suman

www.beastquest.co.uk

ORCHARD BOOKS
338 Euston Road, London NW1 3BH
Orchard Books Australia
Level 17/207 Kent St, Sydney, NSW 2000

A Paperback Original
First published in Great Britain in 2010

Beast Quest is a registered trademark of Beast Quest Limited
Series created by Working Partners Limited, London

Text © Beast Quest Limited 2010
Cover and inside illustrations by Steve Sims © Orchard Books 2010

A CIP catalogue record for this book is available
from the British Library.

ISBN 978 1 40830 735 9

1 3 5 7 9 10 8 6 4 2

Printed in Great Britain by CPI Bookmarque, Croydon

The paper and board used in this paperback are natural recyclable
products made from wood grown in sustainable forests. The
manufacturing processes conform to the environmental regulations of
the country of origin.

Orchard Books is a division of Hachette Children's Books,
an Hachette UK company.

www.hachette.co.uk

CRETA
THE WINGED
TERROR

BY ADAM BLADE

ORCHARD BOOKS

THE ICY

THE NORTHERN
MOUNTAINS

TH

WESTERN OCEAN

THE FOREST
OF FEAR

T

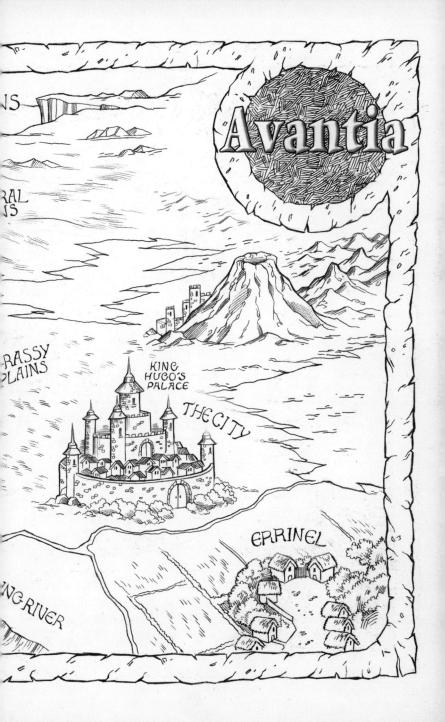

THE DEADLY SWARM

Dear Reader,

We should have known that Malvel's evil would not be kept at bay for long. Though he has not been seen within Avantia's shores, his power still lurks in dark places. My heart tells me that a new menace is coming – an ancient curse that Avantia has not faced for hundreds of years. I have no doubt that Malvel is behind it.

Thank goodness we have a hero to face such magic, even if he is only a boy. If anyone can stop Malvel, it's Tom, son of Taladon. But I fear that even he might not have the strength to face this threat.

Follow Avantia's bravest young hero on this special mission.

Read if you dare.

Marc, apprentice wizard to Aduro

CHAPTER ONE

THE COMING OF THE SWARM

Tom rolled over onto his back with a sigh of contentment. He linked his hands behind his head and stared up at the sky. The stars glittered like diamonds in the black velvet night, and the half-moon cast its soft light on the mountainside. From up here, Tom could see the whole of Avantia spread out in a silvery glow. His stomach was full and he felt rested.

Avantia is safe from the menace of the Beasts, he thought. *And best of all, I'm camping in the mountains with my father.*

Taladon, Avantia's Master of the Beasts, had once been a prisoner of Malvel, but Tom had rescued him. Now, he lay sleeping in the orange glow of the campfire; his weathered face was calm. Tom tried to imagine how it had been for his father, trapped by the evil magician for all those years, as Tom grew up.

Tom wiped his forehead; it was a humid night. He kicked off his blanket and tried to get more comfortable on the stony ground. He felt something crawling on his skin and he swatted it away. *Dratted annoying mosquitos*, he thought to himself.

Feeling excited, Tom turned his thoughts to the following day. Taladon was taking him fishing on the Western shore. Sepron, Avantia's sea serpent and protector of the shore, lived there in the depths. Tom wondered if he and his father would see the great Beast as they fished for mackerel and sea trout. It felt like such a long time since Tom had freed Sepron from Malvel's enchantments.

Again, Tom felt something crawling on his skin. Sitting up, he brushed it away irritably. The creature fell off his arm and landed on the ground.

"Urgh!" Tom exclaimed. He backed away with a grimace. He could see that the creature was some kind of cockroach. Its black shell gleamed like oil in the moonlight. When it opened its wing-cases, Tom caught a glimpse of silver, and a putrid stench rose up.

As he watched the bug fly away, he let out a gasp – the ground was crawling with thousands of insects, and some were on him! Silent creatures scuttled across the packed dirt, making the ground swell and ebb like an ocean. Several were creeping on the sleeping form of

Taladon, their little feet pattering across his body. Their wing-cases clicked softly as they moved. Tom jumped to his feet.

"Father…" he called, trying to keep calm. "Wake up!"

Yawning, Taladon opened his eyes. When he saw the bugs he quickly leapt up and swatted at himself.

The creatures pattered to the ground. The noise of their clicking wing-cases grew louder.

"What are they?" Tom said in disgust as the creatures scuttled around his feet.

Taladon snatched a bug off his shoulder and held it carefully in his calloused hands. "I don't know," he said, sounding puzzled. "I've never seen anything like it before."

The creature clicked its wings, scrambling around Taladon's hands. Two pale eyes gleamed in its armoured body.

"Get rid of it," said Tom uneasily. "There's something...evil about it."

Taladon released the bug. It fell to the ground and joined the rest of the swarm. On the far side of the glowing embers of the campfire, Storm and

Fleetfoot – Tom and Taladon's horses – tossed their heads. They neighed and stamped their hooves, knocking several bugs off their legs.

The clicking of the creatures' wings became unbearably loud; suddenly they took off. The sound of their wings burst over Tom and Taladon's heads like a wave. Tom ducked, brushing the top of his head as they skimmed close to his scalp. Then, as quickly as they'd arrived, they were gone.

"Good riddance," said Taladon.

Something about the little winged creatures unsettled Tom. He went to calm Storm and Fleetfoot. The two stallions were pressed close together, shivering.

"The smoke from the fire will drive the swarm off if they try and come back," said Taladon, adding dry kindling to the embers of the campfire and blowing on it. He tossed on several pieces of green wood to create extra smoke.

Soon grey clouds swirled in the night sky. Tom squinted into the moonlight, but there was no sign of the bugs. After a few moments, he settled back down beside the fire with his father, who swiftly drifted back to sleep. Tom watched the smoke dreamily. It seemed to be moving…taking shape…

Tom's eyes widened. There in the smoke was the face of his friend Elenna. Elenna and her wolf, Silver, had accompanied Tom on his Quests. She looked worried.

"Tom?" Elenna's voice echoed. "Can you see me?"

"I'm here, Elenna," said Tom.

Taladon sat up at the sound of Tom's voice. Now he too saw the face in the smoke.

"Marc has sent me to give you an important message." Elenna's voice sounded strained. "Avantia is suffering from some sort of…*infestation*. It…it's hard to describe, but…"

"Bugs?" Tom guessed.

Elenna looked surprised. "How do you know?" she said. "They're all over the castle here, and we've heard about swarms in the town."

"We have them here as well," said Tom. "Horrible shiny things with black wing-cases. They must be spreading fast if they've come this far into the mountains."

"Yes!" said Elenna. "They give me the creeps. I don't know why…"

Elenna's voice trailed away. Tom knew exactly what she meant. Even though they had faced huge and terrifying Beasts together, there was something deeply sinister about these tiny clicking creatures.

"Please," Elenna said. "We need you and Taladon to return to King Hugo's castle at once. The kingdom needs your help!"

Tom thought about the Western shore, and the fishing rods in Storm and Fleetfoot's packs. Pushing the thought away firmly, he nodded. "We'll saddle up at first light and come back," he promised.

Elenna's face faded from the smoke. Taladon put his hand on Tom's shoulder.

"Avantia needs us again," he said.

Tom nodded. "There'll be another time for this trip."

As the sun's first rays filtered over the mountain tops, Tom and Taladon saddled up and galloped down the mountainside towards King Hugo's castle.

Whatever the threat, we'll face it, Tom thought. *With my father by my side, we're unbeatable.*

CHAPTER TWO

STABIORS

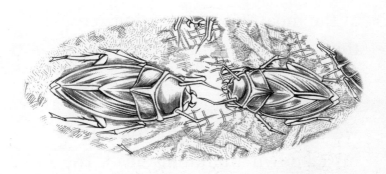

Tom and Taladon pulled up their
horses at the gates of the castle.
Sweat stuck Tom's shirt to his back.
Even though it was dawn, it already
felt as hot as midday. Something was
terribly wrong.

The stinking air above the castle
was black with swarming insects.
Tom could hear the insistent clicking
of their wings overhead. He shuddered;

the sound was horrible. Dismounting, Tom led Storm to a nearby water trough. Fleetfoot joined them.

As the horses drank, Tom glanced at the moat. It was steaming gently in the heat.

Tom frowned at the great golden walls surrounding the castle. They were pockmarked with holes. Dust hissed down around his head. The castle walls were crumbling!

"There's been a bombardment!" Taladon gasped. "Who would attack King Hugo in this way?"

Tom wondered if his father was right. The pockmarks looked fresh, but there was no enemy to be seen – no siege towers, no weapons, nothing that could have caused the damage. He looked closer. *The walls themselves were swarming with bugs, eating away at the stonework!* The insects' wing-cases glittered in the dawn light. The clicking sounds of millions of bugs sent a chill down Tom's back. He couldn't see anybody on the battlements.

"Cannon fire didn't make those holes," Tom said. He hurried over to the gate and banged hard on the door. "What's happening here?" he called.

There was no answer. The chittering sound of the insects filled the air. Tom knocked again, harder. A small window slid open and a pair of terrified eyes gazed out at them.

"Get away from here," hissed the sentry. "Run away! The castle is all but lost!"

"Has there been an invasion?" Taladon demanded, striding up to the window.

The sentry's eyes flickered as he recognised Tom and Taladon. "The swarm," he whispered. "It's eating the walls. And the grain supply, too! It's eating everything it can find."

"Let us in," Tom demanded. "King Hugo wants to see us immediately."

As the gate swung back on its iron hinges, Tom and Taladon strode into the courtyard, leading their horses. Everywhere, soldiers and castle dwellers were doing their best to shore up the crumbling walls. Poles, pitchforks, furniture – everything was piled high, braced against the unstable stone. The rotting smell of the insects was all around.

"Help us!" called a man frantically. "The walls might come down at any moment!"

Soldiers and castle dwellers rushed towards Tom and Taladon. Tom found himself surrounded.

"The swarm is everywhere... All hope is lost!" A powerfully built soldier strode through the crowd and

stood before Tom and Taladon. Tom
recognised him at once. It was
Captain Harkman, commander of
King Hugo's troops.

"The king is in the throne room,"
said Harkman. He looked tired, his
red hair dark with sweat. Harkman
was a tough man; Tom remembered

him from his brief training with the Avantian army. If Captain Harkman looked weary, things were serious.

"Aduro is there as well," Captain Harkman added.

Tom nodded. It was good to know that Aduro was in the castle. He had the feeling they would need the help of King Hugo's wizard more than ever. He wondered if Elenna was with the king, too.

Tom patted Storm and handed his reins to a wide-eyed stable boy. "Stable him with plenty of cool water and a full hay net," he instructed. "Take my father's horse, too." Then he broke into a run, heading past the golden tower towards the castle.

Tom and Taladon raced up the stone steps to the vast oak doorway, through the Great Hall and on up the sweeping stairs to the throne-room itself. They burst in before the startled guards on the throne-room door had time to announce the visitors. Aduro rose to greet them. In the corner, Elenna gave a strained smile. Aduro's assistant, Marc, raised a hand, looking relieved to see Tom and Taladon.

"Welcome, Tom and Taladon," said King Hugo in a grim voice. "I'm sorry you arrive in such circumstances."

Tom bowed. Beside him, his father did the same. They heard the unpleasant clicking sound of the bugs again. Tom looked around and realised that insects were climbing the walls of the throne-room, their tiny eyes glinting with evil delight. The precious tapestries were disintegrating as Tom watched, eaten

up by the stinking bugs that swarmed
over them.

"What *are* these things?" Taladon exclaimed, waving a hand towards the bugs.

Elenna came forward. Her wolf, Silver, stood by her side. "Stabiors," she said.

Tom frowned. *I've never heard of them*, he thought.

"Stabiors?" Taladon said. "Didn't they leave Avantia years ago?"

"I was attacked while hunting in the forest with Silver," Elenna explained. "When I saw their wing-cases and heard the noise they made, I knew at once what they were. My uncle used to tell us scary stories about them. I ran to raise the alarm here at the palace. Now they are everywhere."

"But stabiors left Avantia years ago!" Taladon said. "I'm sure of it!"

"Well, they're back," said Aduro soberly.

Everyone gazed up at the creatures on the throne-room walls. There were hundreds of them. *Thousands*.

"Urgh!" Marc leaped to one side, brushing at his shoulders. Three evil-looking bugs clattered to the flagstone floor.

King Hugo ran his finger around his collar. Tom was made aware of the sweat forming on his own neck. The heat was growing more oppressive. He swatted a Stabior away as it buzzed close to his face.

"This isn't natural," said Tom slowly.

Aduro nodded his head.

"*Malvel*." Tom guessed. "Is that who's done this?"

Everyone fell silent at the mention of the evil magician's name.

"He has to be behind the swarm," said Tom. "But where is the heat coming from?"

"We don't know why it is so hot," Marc admitted. "Stabiors don't generate heat."

Creeeaak! A terrible groaning from outside sent everyone to the throne-room window. They watched helplessly as the huge golden tower,

now black with insects, shook before their eyes. The ground shuddered. There was a deafening sound of crumbling stone and shattering glass.

"It's going to—" Elenna cried out. But it was too late. The tower was already falling.

CHAPTER THREE

THE CAPTAIN IS MISSING!

The noise was horrifying as the tower collapsed. Enormous stones cascaded into the courtyard and people scattered like ants. A young man fell to the ground, blood pouring down his face. The screams and wails of the injured floated up to the throne-room window.

Tom hurtled out. He took the stone

steps down to the Great Hall three at a time, his father and Elenna at his side. He was aware of the king, Aduro and Marc following close behind.

In the courtyard, the rubble of the tower was settling. Dust plumed and people limped past Tom with gashes on their arms and legs. Soldiers ran in all directions, covered in dust.

"Is anyone missing?" Tom called urgently.

The sentry who had been on guard duty swayed towards him. "I can't find the captain, sir," he said in a dazed voice.

After a quick search, King Hugo strode towards Tom through the swirling dust. "It's true," he said. "Captain Harkman has disappeared."

"We'll sort through the rubble," Elenna said. "The captain may be trapped underneath. Come on, Silver! We need your nose."

As the great wolf bounded over, Tom shuddered. If the captain had been hit by the falling tower, it was almost certain that he was dead.

Clouds of Stabiors flew in black clouds above the courtyard as Tom, Taladon and the others searched for the captain. They pulled at chunks of stone and rolled them aside as best they could. It was hot work, made worse by the buzzing of the insects.

"Silver can't pick up a scent through the stench of the Stabiors," Elenna panted, standing back from the rubble at last.

"If Captain Harkman isn't beneath the tower," said the king with a frown, "where is he?"

They searched the courtyard again.

Aduro sent men into the castle to see
if Harkman had taken refuge inside.
Marc muttered incantations,
sweeping his wand around the castle
walls. But the captain was nowhere
to be found.

"Is it possible that the captain has deserted?" Tom asked. It seemed unlikely.

Taladon shook his head. "I've known Harkman for many years," he said. "He's a hard man to like, but he's always been brave and true to King Hugo. He would never desert at a time like this."

It's almost as if Captain Harkman has vanished into thin air, Tom thought.

Tom looked down as something scurried past his foot. It was the ferret belonging to King Hugo's Master-of-Arms. The ferret stood on its back legs and squeaked in alarm. Then it bounded away.

The ferret never deserted his Master! Tom shared a look with his father.

"Something's wrong in the chamber," said Tom.

"The Golden Armour!" he and Taladon exclaimed together.

The Master-of-Arms guarded Avantia's magical Golden Armour. Each piece was endowed with magical powers. It had once been taken by the Dark Wizard Malvel and scattered across the kingdom. Tom and Elenna had brought it back, piece by piece, on a Quest. Surely it hadn't been taken again?

Tom spun around and ran towards the tower where the armour was kept. Taladon ran beside him. They rushed through a door at the base of the armoury, then along the stone corridor towards the spiral stairs which led down to the chamber where the armour was kept.

The stout, padded door to the chamber was locked from the inside, and there was no sound coming from within.

"Look," said Tom, and pointed at the bottom corner of the door.

Part of the solid oak had been chewed away, leaving a large gap. Tom looked at the rest of the door more closely. It was riddled with holes amid the brass studs that held the leather padding in place. The Stabiors had devoured it.

"We could try to push it open," Taladon suggested.

Tom nodded. "On the count of three," he said. "One…two…three!" Tom and his father rammed their shoulders at the door. Splinters of chewed oak spun away from the door frame, but the door did not move.

"Again!" Tom called. "One…two… *three*."

It was more than the weakened
door could take. With a squeal of
protest, it broke away from its hinges
and clattered to the ground. They'd
done it!

Among the polished cabinets where the king's weapons and armour were kept, the body of the Master-of-Arms lay face down, sprawled on the floor. The stand which held the Golden Armour was empty.

Tom knelt down and felt the Master's neck. At first, there was nothing. He looked at Taladon and shook his head. Then a faint pulse fluttered under his fingertips. Tom's heart leaped as the Master groaned weakly and rolled over. He was clutching the golden breastplate to his chest.

"What happened here?" Taladon asked, helping the Master to his feet.

The ferret was back, slinking up the Master's body. "The Stabiors," gasped the Master-of-Arms, holding his side.

"They entered through the door and came at me. At first, they didn't worry me. They couldn't harm the armour. The worst I thought could happen was that they might fill the place with their stench and make the armour dirty. But then…"

The Master dropped his head, fighting for breath. His ferret settled on his shoulder.

"We should get you a chair to sit on," Tom suggested.

Taladon went to get a stool, but the Master shook his head.

"The Stabiors," he continued with difficulty. "I couldn't believe what I saw. They began to carry pieces of the armour across their backs in organised groups. They were like ants, taking food to their nests. I tried to lock them out, but..."

He pointed at the remains of the armoury door. "Well," he said. "You can see for yourselves. A locked door was nothing to these creatures. They chewed their way through."

"But why did you pass out?" Taladon wanted to know.

The Master-of-Arms shuddered with disgust. "They swarmed all over me," he said with a gulp. "On my face. My nose. My mouth... I couldn't breathe! I grabbed the breastplate, I remember, but then everything went black." He groaned. "I have failed to protect what is most precious to Avantia," he said. "So much of the armour is gone. The king will be angry."

Tom shook his head. "Malvel doesn't have the *whole* suit of armour," he reminded the Master-of-Arms. "You've done well. King Hugo will understand. This is no ordinary swarm; evil is at work here."

"Malvel," said Taladon softly.

"But why would Malvel try to take the armour again?" Tom asked his father.

"To weaken us," Taladon said. "Destroy our confidence."

The Master-of-Arms covered his face.

Tom felt a wave of anger break over him. "While there's blood in my veins," he vowed aloud, "Malvel won't get away with this!"

CHAPTER FOUR

INSECT ARMOUR

Tom gazed at the closed throne-room
door. King Hugo had locked himself
away since hearing about the loss
of the precious armour. Tom was left
to pace the corridor outside with
Elenna, Taladon and the two
magicians.

How much longer? Tom thought.
They had to act fast, or the whole
castle would meet the same fate as

the golden tower.

Silver snapped at one of the bugs as it buzzed around his head. Breaking away from Elenna's side, he bounded down the corridor, trying to catch the creature in his jaws. Taladon and Aduro stood talking beside the corridor window. The anxiety in their hushed voices was making Tom nervous.

"Your shield is glowing, Tom," said Marc suddenly.

Elenna was by Tom's side in an instant. Tom stopped pacing and swung his shield off his back. He studied the six tokens embedded in its battle-scarred surface.

Epos's talon was glowing.

Epos was one of Avantia's six great Beasts, a huge phoenix with blood-red wings and awesome powers. She lived in the Stonewin Volcano in eastern

Avantia. When Tom liberated her from an evil spell cast by Malvel, Epos had given him the talon – with it, Tom could call on Epos whenever he needed her. But he hadn't called. The glowing talon could only mean one thing.

Epos needed *him*.

"We have to go to Epos," said Tom, lifting his shield onto his back.

The throne-room door swung open just as Tom and Elenna were breaking into a run. Tom turned and bowed hastily to King Hugo.

"Begging your leave, Your Majesty," said Tom. "But Epos is calling us."

"Go then, Tom," said King Hugo soberly. "And you, Elenna. With my blessing. In Stonewin, there may be an answer to whatever is causing this dreadful heat."

The king turned to Tom's father. "Taladon," he said, "I want you to stay and organise the men in Captain Harkman's absence. They know and trust you."

"As you wish, Your Majesty," said Taladon with a bow. He laid his hand on Tom's shoulder. "You don't need me to go to Stonewin with you. I know you and Elenna will help Epos."

Silver's claws clicked on the flagstones, making everyone turn around. The wolf padded up to Elenna, holding something in his mouth. Elenna bent down for a closer look.

"It's a Stabior," she said. "A dead one."

Taking the bug carefully from Silver's mouth, Elenna studied it.

Tom moved in for a closer look. He wrinkled his nose at the smell. The creature's oily black carapace with its silver lining glittered like a living thing. Even in death, its pale eyes still seemed to shine with evil.

Aduro took the insect from Elenna, shuddering at the feel of its brittle armour. He looked troubled.

"Tom and Elenna," he said after a moment. "I need you to follow me."

Tom, Elenna and Silver followed the magician as he strode down the stone steps and out into the courtyard. King Hugo and Taladon remained with Marc.

Tom wondered if Aduro was taking them to his chambers at the top of the tallest turret in the castle, but the magician turned abruptly as they reached the turret door, and walked towards what looked like a solid wall.

The magician reached out a hand and pressed hard against one of the stones. To Tom's astonishment, there was the click of a catch and the wall swung open. Silver barked nervously, backing away with his hackles raised.

"What is this place?" Elenna marvelled, as she and Tom followed

Aduro into the darkness.

"A secret room," Aduro said. He clapped his hands sharply. Flames leaped in the sconces on the walls, lighting the way down some stairs. "It has been here longer than most of the castle."

"What is kept here?" Tom asked.

When they reached the bottom of the stairs, Aduro took a key from his pocket and unlocked the blackened oak door, which screeched back on its hinges.

Four stands covered with ghostly dustsheets were in the dim room. Aduro stretched out his fingertips. Glowing magic snaked through the air, twitching at the sheets. They slid away to reveal four suits of armour.

At first glance, the armour appeared to be made of glittering black metal.

Tom looked more closely. He reached
out and touched the oily surface of
the nearest breastplate before pulling
his hand back sharply.

"Stabiors!" he gasped.

"Stabior *shells*," Aduro corrected.
Elenna ran her hands over the insect
armour in wonder. "Thousands of
them, woven into suits of armour.

No one knows how long these have
been in this room. Our recorded
history doesn't go back far enough.
But clearly they were made for
heroes long gone. They are
exquisitely made."

Tom examined the armour in
disbelief. The craftsmanship was
stunning. He knew at once that the

suits were connected with the new infestation of Stabiors. Had the creatures been hunting for *this* armour, and taken the golden armour in its place?

Aduro reached up for one of the flaming sconces on the wall. Taking it down, he held it to the nearest suit of armour.

"Don't burn it!" Elenna said, starting forward.

Aduro smiled. "It will not burn," he said. "Watch."

The flame from the sconce licked up the armour. Nothing curled, or wilted. Nothing even glowed.

"These not only resist heat," Aduro went on, "they reflect it. As you are going to Epos and the Stonewin Volcano, I think you will find these useful."

"We can *wear* them?" Tom gasped.

"Naturally," smiled Aduro. "They were made for heroes, after all."

Tom and Elenna exchanged excited glances. They each took a suit and put it on. Tom's felt surprisingly light. He tugged experimentally at the breastplate. Nothing yielded.

"To the stables," said Tom. "I need to saddle Storm. Come on, Elenna! Silver! There isn't a moment to lose!"

CHAPTER FIVE

EPOS IN TROUBLE

The terrible heat of the day pressed down on Avantia like a dragon's flame. However, Tom and Elenna felt cool in their strange new armour as they galloped on Storm across the hot stones. Silver loped beside them, his tongue lolling and his coat dark with sweat. They passed villages where the grass lay scorched on the ground, and panting livestock gathered around dwindling wells. The heat was unbearable.

The sun had tracked high in the sky before Tom and Elenna finally dismounted at a shallow stream so they could drink. Silver joined the stallion, dipping his head into the trickling flow. Steam rose ominously from the stream. Elenna scooped up water in her cupped hand and drank.

"It's warm," she said with a grimace.

"Avantia can't take much more of this heat," said Tom. His stomach tingled with fear. "The water will evaporate, just like this stream."

They had no choice but to press on. The Stonewin Volcano glowered on the horizon. The black cone at the top seemed to be shimmering and the shield on Tom's back was vibrating hard. Epos needed him. Tom dug his

heels into Storm's sweating sides and
bent low over the stallion's neck,
with Elenna clinging on behind.

Tom reined Storm in as they reached the village of Rokwin. He glimpsed the dusty brown roofs of Stonewin village to the north.

He and Elenna had both been to Rokwin during their Quest to free Blaze the ice dragon. As Tom dismounted, he saw a familiar tall figure emerging from one of the houses huddled around the central village square.

"Derlot!" Tom exclaimed. He hurried over to greet his old friend as Elenna tethered Storm.

"Back to save us again, Tom?" said Derlot. His tone was humorous as he shook Tom's hand, but he seemed stooped and anxious. Tom could see that his friend looked strained. The air here was so dry and hot that Tom was finding it difficult to swallow.

"There's something wrong with the volcano," said Derlot, wiping his brow. "The ground shook yesterday, and there was a crash near the summit. We felt it all the way down here."

A buzzing Stabior-cloud swooped over their heads. Tom ducked.

"What are those stinking creatures?" Derlot asked with a frown.

"You're better off not knowing," said Elenna grimly.

"They've been buzzing around the top of Stonewin for a couple of days," Derlot told them.

Tom and Elenna looked up at the top of the mountain. The shimmering they'd seen around the volcano's cone wasn't heat, Tom realised. *It's a vast cloud of Stabiors.*

"We have to reach the top of the volcano," said Tom. "Can you look after Storm and Silver for me?"

Derlot nodded. "Is there anything else I can do?" he called after Tom and Elenna, as they made their way to the steep, rocky path that would take them to Epos.

"Be prepared," Tom called back. "For anything!"

With his sword by his side and his

shield lashed firmly to his back, Tom began to climb. Elenna climbed beside him. At first the path ran smoothly, zigzagging up the mountainside. The ground that flanked the path was lush and fertile, planted with the medicinal herbs for which Rokwin was famed. Tom could see that the herbs were beginning to wither and dry out. The heat would destroy everything unless they could bring it under control.

The path started to narrow. Gravel slid beneath Tom and Elenna's feet as the ground grew hotter and drier. *Thank goodness for the armour*, Tom thought. *It's the only thing that's letting us survive*. They walked quickly. The barren crown of the volcano loomed above them. Above that whirled the cloud of Stabiors – and the outline of

Epos the phoenix.

Epos was lying on her side among the detritus of smashed boulders. She raised her fiery head and cried out in pain. One of her wings flapped weakly. The other lay pinned uselessly at her side.

"She's been injured," Elenna gasped. The noise that Derlot had heard must have been the falling boulders.

Making their way quickly up the final stretch of the mountain path, Tom went to Epos's side. The phoenix's great red eyes were clouded with pain and her plumage had lost its fiery colour. Her wing was broken.

As Elenna tried to pull away the rocks that trapped Epos, Tom felt for the six magical jewels set in his belt. Tom's fingers settled on the green jewel he had won in his great battle to free Skor the winged stallion, which healed broken bones.

Tom made his way along the great length of Epos as she lay beside the volcano's crater. The Stabiors buzzed madly around him as he held the jewel against the phoenix's broken wing. The air shimmered with healing magic. Epos's eyes sharpened and focused. Her plumage blazed with fresh fire. With a mighty screech of joy the phoenix raised both her wings and drove herself up into the shimmering sky.

Elenna shaded her eyes and watched, smiling as the phoenix made a loop through the air. Tom moved closer to the volcano's yawning mouth. Instead of seething fire, broken rocks filled the crater.

Stabiors buzzed incessantly around the volcano's summit, their wings clicking and their jaws working. Hundreds of dead insects lay crushed beneath the fallen rocks, their broken black wing-cases shining in the sun. Those Stabiors that had survived the rock fall were still busy eating away the edge of the crater. Tom realised they had blocked the volcano on purpose. *They meant this to happen!*

"No wonder the kingdom is warming up," said Elenna, standing beside Tom and frowning at the blocked crater. "The pressure in the sealed volcano must be incredible. Thank goodness we arrived."

"It can't go on," said Tom slowly. He started to back away. "The heat needs to escape, Elenna. Otherwise there's going to be—"

BOOOOM!

The deafening noise threw Tom and Elenna to the ground. They felt the

earth shake beneath them. Rocks rained down. Tom flung up his shield to protect his companion. The intense heat blew over their armour, and the rocks bounced harmlessly off the shield.

"The lava!" Tom gasped.

Further down the mountain, they saw an ugly red snake of fire burst through the earth. The lava roiled and spewed, blazing with destruction. Then it started down the slope, gathering speed and burning everything in its path. It was heading straight towards...

"Rokwin!" Elenna cried.

CHAPTER SIX

ARCTA TO THE RESCUE

Tom jumped to his feet. They had to outpace the lava and reach Rokwin to warn Derlot and the others. But the lava was so fast.

Too fast.

Tom slid and scrambled down the mountainside. Small rocks bounced against him, winding him and knocking him off course. He felt the lava singeing the back of his neck, which was unprotected by the Stabior-shell armour. Righting himself, he ran on. Elenna ran close beside him, her black armour glittering. Epos wheeled and screeched overhead.

Now they were beside the great snake of lava. It boiled and bubbled, throwing up yellow gobbets of flame. Their armour protected them from most of the extreme heat, but Tom could feel his hands starting to blister. He threw himself at a large rock and tried to push it into the path of the lava.

"If we can divert the flow, we can save Rokwin!" he shouted to Elenna, who immediately joined him. They leaned together and pushed desperately. But they weren't strong enough; the boulder didn't move.

The lava grew brighter, spreading its fiery destruction across the mountainside. Tom could see the tops of the village houses down below.

"Derlot!" Elenna cried in despair. "The villagers!"

Tom hoped desperately that his advice to Derlot – *Be prepared, for anything* – had been enough. "Get down to the village!" he said to Elenna. "Silver and Storm will help. Start evacuating. *Everyone* must leave the village."

Elenna nodded and raced away down the mountainside. Silver

dashed up towards her. Tom watched as the wolf dived off the path and picked up a toddler by the clothes, who had been playing in the fields above the village. The toddler swung in the wolf's jaws, wailing and crying.

"Everyone, run!" Elenna's frantic voice drifted up the mountain. "Quickly! Run, NOW!"

Tom could see that there was no time for the people to take their belongings. Even if they evacuated the entire village, there would be nothing left to return to. No crops, no houses, no livestock – nothing but fire and destruction.

Epos screeched from high in the sky. Tom knew there was nothing the phoenix could do. Who else could help? Who could he turn to?

The answer came as Tom leaned

hopelessly against the unmoving rock and stared at the precious tokens on his shield.

Arcta, the mountain giant. Of course!

Quickly Tom rubbed the eagle feather that Arcta had given him. "Arcta!" he shouted in desperation. "Rokwin needs you!"

He continued down the mountain as fast as he could, scanning the horizon. First Tom heard Arcta's booming steps, mingling with the rumbling of the volcano beneath his feet. Then he saw Arcta's shaggy red head, rising above the mountains. Arcta's feet boomed on the ground as he strode towards Tom, his great chest heaving and panting. The ground shook wildly; the sound was deafening.

"Arcta!" Tom cried joyfully. It was wonderful to see his old friend, but there was no time to celebrate. He touched the red jewel at his belt. He had won it in his Quest against Torgor the minotaur, and it allowed him to communicate with the Beasts. "Throw!" he shouted, miming a throwing action at the lava. "Rocks, anything! We have to divert the lava flow, or the village will be lost!"

Arcta gazed down at Tom from his

great height. Then the giant bent
down. He seized hold of an
enormous boulder and hurled it into
the lava. Molten rock spattered the
mountainside. Flames leapt up.

"Again!" Tom cried, waving his
arms. The lava had almost reached
the fences that divided the fields from
the mountain slopes.

The giant reached down and scooped up an armful of rocks that were all bigger than Tom. He flung them into the lava and slowly but surely, it began to change direction.

The Rokwin villagers stood frozen, watching the great mountain giant flinging rocks and boulders into the deadly lava. Now the flow had turned, moving alongside the backs of the fields. One of the fences marking the edge of the fields went up in a flash of fire. Then another. Arcta doggedly flung rocks into the boiling magma, blocking it and holding it back. Until at last the golden river of molten rock began to solidify, slow and stop.

The people of Rokwin were safe. For now.

CHAPTER SEVEN

THE CAPTAIN RETURNS

The villagers celebrated their escape from the deadly lava flow with wild whoops of joy. Most of the people kept their distance from Arcta. Others stared wide-eyed, as if they couldn't believe what they were seeing. To many Avantians, the Beasts were just a myth. To see a real Beast was overwhelming.

"Tom!" Elenna hurried to his side. "You did it! We couldn't evacuate quickly enough… If you hadn't— I can't imagine… Children would have been burned alive," Elenna said, as Silver licked Tom's hands.

Grinning, Tom wiped the sweat from his forehead. He glanced up at Arcta, the giant he had saved twice from Malvel. The giant's single brown eye gazed down at him through the mass of red hair that covered his face. Arcta would always protect Tom and the people of Avantia, come what may.

"Tom!" Derlot came towards him through the celebrating crowd, leading Storm. His face was creased into a smile. "How can we thank you? You—"

The air filled with a strange hum.

The horizon blackened. A vast thundercloud of Stabiors seemed to come from nowhere. They spiralled up, dizzying and vast; the stench was appalling. Thousands upon thousands of the creatures, glittering and deadly, spread across the whole sky. Villagers screamed and ran inside their houses.

Storm reared up in shock; Elenna remained rooted to the ground, staring fiercely. Arcta stood like stone as the swarm's great black shadow all but blotted out the sun.

Tom gazed up into the swarm. The Stabiors were twisting, moving, changing. Deep in their midst a face took shape. A face Tom knew all too well.

Malvel.

Arcta roared at the sight of his old tormentor. He swiped at the insects with a massive arm, but the Stabiors writhed back into position. There was nothing that Tom, Elenna or the giant could do but watch.

A booming voice echoed across the sky.

"Big mistake, Tom," Malvel hissed. "This is just the beginning. Until you meet Creta, you know nothing of the terror that awaits you. You know nothing of the despair. Creta will destroy you as surely as my Stabiors destroyed King Hugo's castle walls!"

Arcta roared in defiance again, his arms swiping at the clouds of insects, but to no avail. The face of Malvel remained in their midst, smiling nastily.

Tom unsheathed his sword and pointed its tip at Malvel. "Your threats don't frighten me!" he shouted. "I've fought you before, and I'll fight you again. You were banished from this kingdom, and I will never again let you set foot in Avantia. While there's blood in my veins, I'll stand firm for Avantia's sake!"

Malvel threw back his head and laughed. Then he vanished.

Stabiors dropped out of the sky. Now their little clicking bodies were everywhere, swarming across the ground. Arcta retreated as a great column of seething Stabiors began to form – two, three times as tall as Tom. The column sprouted arms. Then it began to spread, mushrooming outwards. A terrifying face appeared: its mouth bristled with fangs, two mighty horns jutted from its head, and smaller ones lined its skull. A pair of huge orange eyes, with pupils like black lightning, gazed at Tom. Tom knew that this was the next Beast he had to face.

Creta was born.

The giant Beast advanced. Tom could see that several pieces of Avantia's golden armour glinted on its limbs.

The remaining villagers scattered as Creta got closer. Arcta shouted, furious at his powerlessness. Tom fumbled for his sword; Creta leaned towards him and opened its mouth.

Tom leapt back in shock. A second face lurked inside Creta's mouth: a human face! A man with red hair, his face twisted in pain and his eyes full of terror.

It was Captain Harkman.

"Help!" the captain cried in desperation. Insects crawled across his face. "I can't bear it… Help me, Tom!"

The captain's agonised face disappeared into the swarm as Creta closed his jaws again. Tom realised what had happened at the castle. Malvel's swarm had kidnapped the captain and trapped him inside this Beast. An unbeatable monster, made

from the whirring bodies of a
hundred thousand insects. A vision
of evil. Even a Beast as powerful as
Arcta had no way of fighting
something like this.

What possible chance could Tom
and Elenna have?

WATER OF LIFE

Dear Reader,

The village is spared a fiery end, but Malvel's plague is far from defeated. What sort of creature would send doom upon the innocent people of Rokwin? I fear he means to bring destruction to all of Avantia. Thank goodness for Tom and his faithful companions. Have they the courage to defeat the Beast that Malvel has sent? Or will this be one challenge too many for Taladon's son?

And poor Captain Harkman – now a puppet at the mercy of Malvel's swarm. His body is trapped inside the swarms of Stabiors that make up the Beast. Tom will have to be vigilant and courageous to overcome Creta and rescue the captain.

Do you dare accompany Tom on his mission?

Marc

CHAPTER ONE

THE BEAST ATTACKS

Staring at the monstrous Beast that stood in front of him, Tom knew this would be a tough Quest. How could he fight a monster like Creta? How could he save Captain Harkman from his horrible fate?

Creta's jaws snapped. Tom caught another glimpse of the captain, tightly bound and desperate in the heart of the Beast.

Arcta was still standing beside Tom in the village square. His gigantic feet were planted like trees on either side of Rokwin's pond. He roared and swiped at Creta with fists like boulders. Leaving a small hole in Creta's side, the Stabiors scattered to avoid the Beast's attack. Buzzing angrily, they swarmed towards Arcta with terrifying speed. Arcta's head disappeared in a cloud of oily black wings; he roared with pain, clawing at his face, staggering from side to side.

Tom held his sword firmly, pointing it at the Beast. Creta lumbered towards him. The air was foul with the stench of the Stabiors and thick with the whirring of their wings.

"Distract him, Elenna!" Tom called as steadily as he could.

Elenna ran towards the monster. Silver loped at her side. She lifted her bow from her back, fitted an arrow to the string and loosed it. The swarm slid away from the arrow and it whistled harmlessly away.

Tom swallowed and gripped his sword more tightly. Was this Beast truly unbeatable? Would the Stabiors simply move away from his blade, as they had done from Elenna's arrow?

As Tom watched, the creature began to change shape. Its front legs

were growing longer and more
pointed. The tips divided and curled
to form opposing pincers. They
slashed the air, lengthening with
deadly intent.

"More arrows, Elenna!" Tom yelled. He stabbed at the whirring creatures with his sword as Elenna let her arrows fly. His blade connected with the Stabiors, glancing off their hard shells. Bugs clattered to the ground as Creta's shattered pincer withdrew. Moments later the Stabiors had launched back into the air. The reformed pincer slashed again at Tom.

Tom was aware of Elenna loosing arrows in quick succession at the Beast. Silver's teeth flashed as the wolf dived and nipped at Creta's legs, only to shake his shaggy head as the insects buzzed in his ears.

Tom threw himself towards the Beast, whirling his sword. His only hope was to scatter the Stabiors and break up the swarm. Creta swatted at him. Tom felt a glancing blow to his left arm. Looking down, Tom saw that the Beast had drawn blood.

The fight was impossible! Tom needed an advantage. But what?

He parried hard, swatting at the insects. He could feel their hard little bodies swarming up his arms and legs. Tom brushed them off his armour as best he could. He couldn't let the Stabiors seize him the way they had taken Captain Harkman.

No sooner had he swatted one arm clear of bugs, more covered the other one. Tom could feel them marching up his back. They reached his neck, their tiny claws digging hard into his skin. He shook his head desperately when he felt them in his hair, tickling his ears. But he had no time to push them away because Creta's pincers were slashing murderously above

him. He fought on, trying to ignore
the creatures as they crawled over his
unprotected lips, his eyelids…

Elenna's arrows whistled past as Tom fought on desperately. The whirring sound of the Stabiors was deafening. Suddenly there was a stinging pain deep in Tom's head. Tom dropped his sword and clapped his hands to his ears.

The voice, when it came, was as cold as ice. It boomed through Tom's head as he fell to his knees.

Now I have you!

Tom's head sang. Malvel's next words chilled him to the bone.

What can you do to defeat me, Malvel hissed, *now that I am inside your head?*

CHAPTER TWO

A BURNING PAIN

"NO!" Tom shouted.

He shook his head violently. Malvel was laughing. The sound trickled through him like poison. How was such a thing possible?

Tom's body rocked and he held his head between his hands.

"Look out!" Elenna screamed.

Tom reacted to the sound of Elenna's voice just in time. Creta's

pincer was hurtling towards him.
Tom rolled away, curling himself into
a tight ball. The serrated edges of the
swarming pincer broke and scattered
on the ground near Tom's throbbing
head. Stabiors swarmed and crawled
around him, their rotten stench
oozing up his nostrils. With a furious
buzz of wings, the pincer was whole
once again. Creta roared. It sensed
triumph and pulled its pincers back
for another attack.

Tom stumbled to his feet and ran
back to where Elenna was still
steadily firing arrows into the
creature's shimmering body.

"Elenna!" Tom shouted. "I can't
win. There's something terribly
wrong! My head… Malvel—"

A great shriek ripped the air. Tom
and Elenna both looked up. Epos was

circling high overhead, behind Creta's line of vision. Her magnificent red wings were spread wide. Heat radiated from her glowing body.

Tom felt relief flood through him,
even as his head continued to ring
with the ghastly sound of Malvel's
laughter. The great Beast of the
volcano would surely be able to help!

Creta was still advancing. It was
intent on cutting Tom to pieces with
its pincers and hadn't noticed Epos.

"Get back, Elenna!" Tom warned.

Silver leapt and pushed Elenna
down as Tom dived to the ground.

The phoenix's attack took Creta
by surprise. As Epos's great red
wings tore through its body, Stabiors
were scattered in all directions. Creta
stumbled. Once more Tom glimpsed
Captain Harkman in the Beast's jaws.
Epos dived again. The swarm-Beast
had no time to rebuild itself. It
buckled with one blow of the
phoenix's mighty talons.

The Stabiors buzzed and screamed
with fury as they were sent whirling
in all directions.

"Epos is winning!" Elenna cried.

She helped Tom to his feet as the phoenix hurtled back up into the sky. The Stabiors gave chase, but they were not fast enough. The buzzing black cloud spread, broke apart, and drifted back down towards Rokwin. Creta was defeated – for now.

Tom shook his head again. Malvel's laughter was fading and a dull ache formed in its place. Tom felt something sliding through his veins. He clutched his stomach as he felt a stabbing pain deep in his guts – a burning sensation, as if he had swallowed fire. For the first time in a long while, Tom felt truly terrified. How could Malvel make him feel this way? What was wrong with him?

He fell, dimly aware that the ground was rushing up to meet him.

Elenna's worried face loomed over
him as he landed on his back. And
then everything went black.

Tom swam up through strange,
burning dreams. The hard ground of
Rokwin was somehow softer. He
opened his eyes and stared up at a
low, beamed ceiling. He was lying in
a bed, stripped of his Stabior-shell
armour. Bright moonlight illuminated
the walls. Someone was holding a
cup to his lips. Tom spluttered feebly
and cool liquid flowed down his
throat.

"Drink," said a familiar voice.

Tom gazed up at his father as
Taladon held the cup to his lips.

"You will feel better," Taladon
promised.

Tom fixed his eyes on his father.
Taladon appeared weary as he lifted
the cup to Tom's lips again. By the
look of him, Taladon had been with
Tom for most of the night.
Obediently, Tom swallowed. The
painful fire in his belly cooled a little.
He noticed with relief that the air
was cooler than it had been before
Stonewin exploded.

All at once, memories rushed at Tom. He closed his eyes in shame as he remembered how Creta had defeated him. He had fainted like a coward, when Avantia had truly needed him.

Yes, Malvel hissed in his head. *It's true, Tom. You have failed. You have let down your precious king and played right into my hands. Nothing can help you now.*

Tom pushed his hands against the sides of his head. He couldn't bear it. He had to force the voice away somehow...

"Tom?" Taladon put down the cup and looked at Tom with confusion in his eyes. "What's wrong?"

Tom shook his head. He was scared, but he wouldn't share his fear with anyone. Not even his beloved father.

Outside, he could hear the insistent sound of the hungry Stabiors, still eating through the walls of the castle.

I'm going mad, Tom thought with a shiver. *I feel as if Malvel is inside me.*

"Where am I?" he whispered.

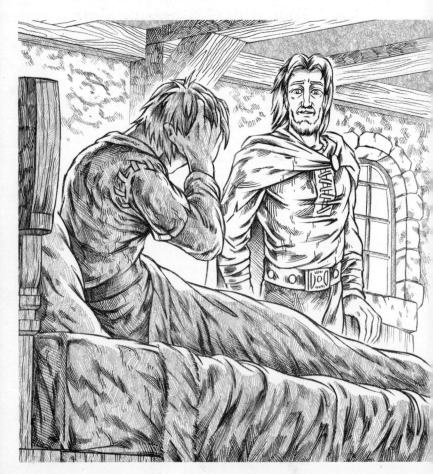

"Back in the castle," said Taladon. "Elenna brought you. Tom, what's the matter? What is this pain?"

Tom shook his head.

Taladon sighed. "You need to rest," he said.

"No," Tom said. "There is no time. I'm not going to let Malvel triumph!"

The pain burned fiercely in his stomach. Tom cried out and Taladon started forward in alarm.

It's too late, mocked the voice in Tom's head. *I already have…*

CHAPTER THREE

THE ONLY HOPE

"Talk to me, Tom!" Taladon said. He took Tom's hand and held it. "I can't help you unless I know what's wrong!"

Inside Tom's head, Malvel was laughing again.

"I'm fine," Tom said. He tried to swing his legs out of the bed, but they felt like jelly. "I just want...to get out of here. Fresh danger, new Beast..." Tom gasped for air. "Creta and the Stabiors will ruin the land unless we do something..." He fell back against the pillow. He felt as weak as a kitten. "And Captain Harkman...trapped inside the Beast!" he whispered. "I can't lie here and let that happen."

The door to the bedchamber flew open. Elenna strode in, Silver by her side. Her face lit up when she saw Tom.

"Elenna," said Tom thankfully. "How did I get here? What happened at Rokwin? Is everyone safe?"

Elenna sat on his bed. "I'm glad to see you're awake," she said. Her voice shook. "I thought you might be dead. I've never seen you like that before. Creta collapsed and the swarm scattered, taking Captain Harkman with it, while I tried to bring you round. When I couldn't, Derlot helped me saddle Storm. We brought you back to the castle. Aduro has visited, but this business with the Stabiors keeps him and the king away. Most of the castle is sleeping now. There is so much to do if we have any hope of saving this place from the Stabiors."

With a great effort, Tom pushed away the echoes of Malvel's laughter.

"We have to saddle Storm and—"

"Storm is injured, Tom," said Elenna soberly. "We can't leave yet."

Tom felt a rush of emotion. His faithful horse! "How?" he demanded, sitting up a little more in the bed.

"It was vital that I got you back here to the castle, so we took the shortest route," Elenna said. "We ran very close to the lava. Too close."

Tom opened his mouth to speak.

"Storm will be fine," Taladon interrupted.

"He was incredibly brave," Elenna added. "Marc has made some special healing ointment for his burns."

Tom sank back weakly. "Thank you, Elenna," he said. "I think you saved my life."

Elenna smiled. "At least the terrible heat has disappeared," she said. "The

Stonewin Volcano is erupting again through the new crater. Thankfully, the lava has followed the same route as the first eruption. Rokwin is still safe."

Tom winced as fiery pain jabbed in his guts again. Elenna reached for the cup that Taladon had left by the bedside and gave it to him. He drank deeply as Taladon lit the oil lamp. The chamber leapt to life in the warm light.

"What's wrong with me?" Tom asked wearily when he had finished drinking.

"I can answer that," said a voice from a dark corner of the room. "Whether you want to hear what I have to say is another matter, Tom."

Tom hadn't noticed Marc sitting in the shadows. A book lay in his lap, its pages fluttering gently in a breeze from the window. The gold decoration on its green leather binding glittered in the moonlight. It was clearly very old.

"I found this volume in Aduro's library," said Marc. "I was looking for something to help us get rid of our plague of Stabiors. Eventually I found a mention of a plague similar to this one – it destroyed a city in the west, where the Great Ruins now stand, in just the same way as these bugs are destroying King Hugo's castle. And it mentions symptoms such as yours. Weakness and…voices?" Marc looked at Tom intently, watching his face. Tom felt his cheeks blush and eventually he nodded, acknowledging Malvel's voice that had embedded itself in his head.

"How can the bugs be stopped?" said Tom.

They can never be stopped, Malvel mocked deep inside his head.

Marc closed the book. "There may be a way," he said. Then he paused and shook his head. "But it seems impossible."

"Tell us," Taladon demanded.

"There is said to be a spring high up in the Shadow Mountains," said Marc. "Its water contains a powerful magic. If we can get some of the water, we may stand a chance against Creta and the Stabiors. But the spring may not even exist."

With a mighty effort, Tom swung his legs out of the bed and stood up. His legs wobbled but he stood as firmly as he could. His stomach burned unbearably. Deep inside his head, Malvel chuckled.

"I have to go to these Shadow Mountains," he said. "Tell me how to get there."

CHAPTER FOUR

UNDER THE SKIN

"Where are these mountains?" said Taladon with a frown. "I've never heard of them."

As Tom ignored the pain in his stomach and hunted for his sword, Marc explained.

"The Shadow Mountains are so remote that no one ever visits them. It's little wonder you don't know them, Taladon. Some people say they don't even exist."

"But *you* are sure they are real, Marc?" Tom checked.

"As sure as I can be, given that I've never been there," Marc said honestly. "They are far in the remote north, on the other side of the River Dour."

Tom thought for a moment. "The other side of the River Dour," he echoed. "That's in Rion…"

"That's right," said Marc. "They're almost permanently shrouded in mist. Most days, the mountains are invisible. Then the mists lift and they drift into view, just long enough for you to wonder if the myths are true: if the water that is said to spring from these mountains does indeed have magical properties. And then the mountains vanish again."

"Has no one ever climbed these

mountains?" asked Elenna.

Tom noticed Marc glance nervously in his direction. "It would be madness," he said with a bitter laugh. "Not only are the mountainsides nearly vertical, but the mists come and go so quickly that you could lose your way – and your life – in an instant."

Silence fell in the castle bedchamber. Tom pulled on his boots, forcing himself to ignore the insistent pain in his belly. It sounded impossible, as Marc had said. But there was no choice. They had to find these mountains, and then track the source of the spring.

And what if the water has no magic? Tom thought before he could stop himself.

Malvel laughed heartily inside his head.

"While there's blood in my veins, I'll find the water and finish Creta and the Stabiors," said Tom through gritted teeth.

Marc stood up. He crossed to Tom and put a hand on his shoulder. "It's time for you to know what's happened to you," the young magician said quietly. "The Stabiors have laid their eggs inside you, Tom. If you don't drink some of this water yourself, you'll soon be just like Captain Harkman. You may not be held by the swarm, but you will be under the Beast's control all the same. And if that happens, Avantia has no chance."

Tom had not imagined anything as bad as this. He closed his eyes and tried not to retch at the thought of the Stabior eggs inside him. He remembered when he had fought up close with the Beast...the stinging pain in his ear... He needed to fight Creta, but first he had to do battle with himself.

"Tom!" Elenna gasped in horror.

Tom looked down. Things were rippling beneath his skin. Living things. *Stabiors*. He could feel new insects hatching in his bloodstream, crawling along his itching bones...

The pain was becoming unbearable. Malvel's voice was still in his head, getting louder. The two things were connected. There wasn't much time.

Tom forced himself to speak calmly. "How can we reach the spring without Storm?" he asked.

"My magic will help you," said Marc. "I haven't quite perfected it, but I can try and send you to the Shadow Mountains."

"You can't send us straight to the spring?" Elenna asked, looking worried.

Marc looked apologetic. "I've done my best," he said. "But I don't have Aduro's experience. Aduro can't help because he is using all his magic to deflect the worst of the Stabior attacks on the castle."

There was a clattering sound as a

Stabior hit the bedchamber window. It scurried across the glass, seeking a way in. The moonlight cast its huge, hideous shadow on the wall behind Taladon's head.

Tom tore his eyes from his crawling, creeping skin. "What do we have to do, Marc?" he asked steadily.

Marc opened his mouth to explain.

"Wait," said Taladon suddenly. "Take the golden breastplate, Tom. Although we only have one piece of golden armour left, it can still protect you better than the Stabior-shell armour you wore against Creta, and it will give you the strength of heart you need to see through this difficult task."

You will need more than strength of heart, Malvel said softly in Tom's head.

Ignoring the evil wizard, Tom reached for the piece of armour that his father was holding out to him. It was a great honour. Tom had once worn the golden armour, but it truly belonged to Taladon.

As Tom slipped it on, he could feel the breastplate's courage flowing into him. He fought back the nausea as the Stabiors squirmed beneath his skin.

Elenna fixed the straps that held the breastplate in place. She looked exhausted.

"You don't have to join me on this Quest, Elenna," said Tom, turning to look at his friend.

"Silver and I follow you wherever you go," Elenna replied. "You should know that by now, Tom." She quickly put on her Stabior-shell armour.

"Good luck, son," said Taladon, and gripped Tom's hand tightly. "And you Elenna."

Marc chanted an incantation and the bedchamber began to swirl away into thick mist. Tom wondered if he would ever see his father again.

The mists cleared and Tom and Elenna found themselves in a strange, grey world.

CHAPTER FIVE

THE SHADOW MOUNTAINS

Tom just had time to catch a glimpse of a towering granite cliff ahead before the mist closed around him again. The whiteness deadened everything. Tom stretched out his hand, and lost sight of his fingers. He'd never known a mist so thick. There was something menacing about it, as if the cloud were squeezing Tom to nothing.

"Elenna?" he called.

The mist dulled his voice to a whisper. Sweeping his arms around, Tom moved forwards. He remembered what Marc had said about vertical cliffs, and travellers who could fall to their deaths in one terrible moment. He remembered the cliff he'd seen ahead of him. It was terrifyingly steep. Clearly they were in some kind of gorge. Through the swirling clouds, Tom could hear the thunder of water.

Tom shuffled forwards carefully. The pain in his stomach was spreading. He could feel the Stabiors multiplying inside him. Trying not to look at his seething skin, Tom felt the spongy ground beneath his feet slope downwards. Through the mist, Tom glimpsed water. He stepped back quickly. From the thundering sound in the air, this was a powerful river. Tom didn't want to risk falling into its foaming depths.

"Elenna!" he called again, louder this time.

"Tom!"

Elenna's voice was thin, but distinct. Tom stretched out his hands, feeling through the damp foggy air.

"Over here!" he shouted. "There's a river… Be careful!"

The mist lifted a little. At last, Tom saw Elenna. She was carefully making her way across the marshy ground towards him, glancing warily from side to side as she moved. Water seeped around her boots and glittered on the Stabior-shell armour she still wore. The mist wrapped around

Silver as he walked beside her. His pale grey coat faded in and out of the fog.

The mist drifted, revealing more of the gorge. Grey cliffs loomed behind and ahead of them, their jagged tops lost in cloud. Crashing between the cliffs, just in front of them, was a tumbling river. It wasn't as wide as Tom had expected, although the current boiled and white water sprayed high into the air.

"How can a river as narrow as that make a gorge as huge and steep as this?" Elenna asked, stopping by Tom's side.

Tom listened to the roar of the water in a haze of pain. It was coming from something much greater than this river. He turned and looked further up the gorge.

A white sheet of water plunged
downwards. A huge waterfall! The
water was dazzling, even in the dim
light of the fog. Everything was
cascading down the grey cliff and
crashing into a deep, foaming pool.

"The source!" Elenna cried exultantly. "The myths about its magical powers must be true. Marc is a miracle worker. We made it, Tom!"

"Not yet," Tom said through gritted teeth. He pointed at the treacherous stretch of marsh and rocks between them and the glittering pool. "When the mist comes down again, this will be impossible to cross."

Elenna started forwards and Silver leapt ahead, sure-footed and confident. "Then there's no time to lose," she called back over her shoulder. "Come on!"

Tom moved slowly after Elenna. With a groan, he suddenly stopped and pressed his hands to his head.

What desperation, Malvel crooned. *What despair! To come to this cursed place... There is no hope, Tom. None at all...*

Tom's eyes were watering from the pain shooting through his belly and limbs. He concentrated on drawing strength of heart from the golden breastplate, which felt warm against his chest. The fog was thickening and he was already losing sight of Elenna. There was no way to tell whether Creta was nearby. The crash of the waterfall would drown out the clicking of Stabior wings. But when Malvel laughed...Tom knew danger wasn't far away.

Elenna was suddenly at his side again.

"Can you go on?" she asked.

Tom nodded wearily.

"I'll carry your shield," Elenna suggested. She lifted it gently away from him. Tom felt lighter, although it was strange not having his trusty shield strapped to his back.

You are a weakling, Malvel taunted.
*You can't even carry your precious shield.
Time is running out, Tom. You are
MINE...*

Tom staggered after Elenna. Silver
ran back and forth, pushing at Tom
with his nose. The ground was
scattered with slick rocks that made
them slip and stumble. Pools of
marsh water sucked at their feet. The
crash of the waterfall was getting
louder.

Tom knew he couldn't go on for
much longer. He staggered towards
the edge of the river, knelt down and
scooped some of the water into his
mouth. The pain eased a little, but
not for long. Tom closed his eyes and
drank some more. The creatures
inside him briefly stopped squirming.

If only the fire would ease… They weren't far from the pool now, he knew it… But how could he continue when he just wanted to fall to the ground?

A foul smell hit his senses and one word formed in Tom's mind: Creta. Opening his eyes, he stared into the water. Then he glimpsed the reflection of a great black pincer as it rushed towards him. With all his strength, Tom rolled away. Creta's great claw crashed into the rocks where his neck had been moments earlier.

The gorge boomed with the noise of Creta's fury. Stabiors whirled above Tom's head. The creatures beneath his skin stirred once again, woken by the sound of their brothers.

"Elenna!" he croaked. "Creta is here!"

Elenna drifted into view for a brief
moment as Creta lifted his evil head.
His horns were murderous. His
pincers slashed this way and that as
he leapt towards Tom. The black slits
in the Beast's eyes loomed, wide and
dark as caves as he opened his jaws.

Suddenly, Creta stumbled. With a ghastly shriek, the Beast split in half as something flashed through its middle. With a dull thud, Tom's shield landed on a rock. Elenna had flung it as hard as she could at the monster.

The Stabiors swarmed, disorientated and angry, then flew away among the rocks. The stench was awful and overpowering. There was no sign of the captain in their midst. Creta was gone – at least for now.

Tom crawled on all fours towards his shield. It seemed so far away. He reached unsteadily for it. "Thank you," he managed.

"I can't leave you alone for a minute, can I?" Elenna grinned.

Tom fastened his shield onto his back again. "Creta will return," he said. "We have to keep going."

They pressed on. The going was slow. The waterfall and its glittering pool taunted them, flickering in and out of sight in the dancing mist.

Next time Creta appeared, Tom was ready. The Beast poured upwards out of the ground, Scabior wings buzzing in fury. Tom slammed his shield into the only part of Creta not protected by the golden armour: its black, buzzing chest. Creta staggered backwards, caught by surprise, and lost its balance.

It roared with pain as one huge foot entered the foaming river. The water hissed and boiled. Tom could see dead Stabiors dropping away as Creta staggered ashore again.

A glimmer of hope surged through
Tom's pain. The water *was* harmful to
the creature! But not lethal. Not yet.

"If we can somehow get the Beast
into the pool, the battle will be won,"
he shouted to Elenna.

It was the only way.

CHAPTER SIX

THE POWER RETURNS

Tom had to stop every few paces to drink. His knees were giving way. He couldn't go on much longer. Creta nipped and swung at him. Tom kept going doggedly.

"Keep close…to the river," Tom panted to Elenna. He fell to his knees. He could barely move. "The Beast…won't come close…"

Creta was keeping a wary distance from the glittering water. Stabiors broke away from the Beast and dived at Tom and Elenna. Their black wings whirred close to Tom's face, blinding him. Their rotting smell was everywhere. Tom pushed the creatures away.

Ahead of Tom, Elenna swiped at the foul creatures buzzing around her head. Silver was jumping at the insects, snapping angrily and shaking his grey head as they darted and nipped at his ears. One or two Stabiors lay dead on the rocks as Tom crawled onwards.

"Arghh!"

Elenna had slipped and fallen into a marshy pool a little way ahead. The water sucked hungrily at her as she sank to her waist in the slime and mud. Her gaze widened with terror as she realised she was sinking.

"Don't struggle," Tom mumbled. "It…makes it worse…"

Panting, he crept closer and reached out his hand. Elenna seized it. Pain exploded around Tom's eyes like fireworks as he worked steadily to drag at Elenna until she burst free. Stabiors dive-bombed them from all directions.

"You're doing well!" Elenna cried, helping Tom onwards towards the pool. "Really well, Tom. We're nearly there. Nearly there…"

Elenna's voice was beginning to fade from Tom's head. All he could hear was Malvel's laughter. It boomed through him. It roared. Spots danced before his eyes.

Tom scooped feebly at the water. The crippling fire in his limbs was threatening to overcome him.

You won't make it, Malvel laughed. Tom closed his eyes. He looked deep inside himself. With all his strength, he drew on the power of the golden breastplate. Courage pushed him onwards.

And then suddenly Tom could feel the spray of the waterfall on his face. He lifted his head and welcomed the icy sensation on his skin. Opening his eyes again, he was dazzled. Light seemed to pour from the water itself. Elenna cupped her hands. Water splashed into her palms.

"Diamonds!" she said in a hushed voice, gazing down as they ran through her fingers. Silver barked madly. "This water contains *diamonds*, Tom!"

Half-blind with pain, Tom gazed at the crashing water. He could see the glitter of the diamonds: the hardest known substance. The crystals wore relentlessly away at the granite. No wonder the gorge was so deep.

He crawled on, past Elenna, towards the very base of the great cliff. There was a ledge right at the bottom of the waterfall. Water bounced there before crashing into the deep pool. If he could reach it… If he could just lie there and let the cooling water soak him through. Then he could face the Beast; Creta was waiting somewhere. Waiting. Watching…

Stabiors swarmed overhead, afraid to come too close to the shining water. Tom pulled himself onto the ledge with one final effort. The water pounded down on him, threatening to push him into the pool. He held on, passing through the gleaming cascade. He rolled onto his back on the wet ledge. It was all he could do to open his mouth.

Water poured into him. Tom felt its cleansing power as Malvel screamed with fury.

AAAAAAGGHHHH!

The evil magician's cry of anger began to fade. Tom gulped greedily. *Aaaaaahhh...*

Water crashed over Tom's body. It drenched him. It coursed through him. The creatures inside him became still, and fell silent. The burning ceased.

The curse was gone.

Tom sprang to his feet. He felt more alive than he could ever remember. The water had filled him with energy. Now he was ready to finish this Quest!

Tom pushed through the dazzling waterfall to stand on the ledge. He planted his legs firmly on the granite. His breastplate shone like fire in the glittering water. Down by the edge of the pool, he could see Elenna fighting off the Stabiors. Silver growled and clawed the air. Elenna caught sight of

Tom and almost lost her footing at the pool's edge. Tom saluted her, smiling. She smiled back, and managed a brief wave before a fresh storm of Stabiors demanded her attention.

Creta prowled around the far side of the pool, swinging his vile spiked head and grunting with rage. Tom saw that it could come no closer. The waterfall spray burned it like fire.

Tom swung his sword tauntingly at Creta. Unstrapping his golden breastplate, Tom held it out, over the glittering pool. It was the only piece of armour that he had. If Creta took it, Malvel would win.

"It's here if you want it, Creta!" he shouted, swinging the breastplate like bait. "All you have to do is come and get it!"

The Beast's yellow eyes fixed on the breastplate, but it didn't move. Creta was too clever for that and knew the water would hurt it.

An idea hit Tom like lightning. If Creta wouldn't come to the water, he would have to take water to the Beast. He thrust his sword into the cascading water behind him. The magical liquid coated the steel; the lustre from the wet blade was blinding.

Tom jumped lightly down from the ledge, his sword dripping magical water.

It was time for the final reckoning.

CHAPTER SEVEN

THE END OF
THE BEAST

Tom strode towards Creta. The
Beast's black pupils narrowed to
vicious slits.

"Scared of the water, are you?"
Tom shouted. He waved his sword.
"Looks like I'll have to bring it to
you!"

The Beast moved like lightning, its
pincers crashing towards Tom. Tom

whirled his sword – and missed. Stabiors buzzed, a vile blackness in the white fog that still blanketed the gorge. Tom spun around, brought his sword flashing back towards the Beast. Again, the Beast's scaly skin parted and knitted back together as Tom's blade passed harmlessly through.

Creta lowered its horns and charged. Tom danced out of the way, throwing himself sideways as the Beast barrelled towards him. The sound from the Stabiors was deafening. The magical water was dripping from Tom's sword. He had to make contact before it ran off the blade completely.

At last, Tom felt his sword connect with Stabiors. Bugs rained down, their shells cleaved in half by his sharp blade and hissing gently as the

water burned them away to nothing.
Elenna cheered as Creta staggered.
One of its pincers was broken into
pieces. Tom raised his sword again.

Blackness descended. Stabiors were swarming across Tom's head, before his eyes and through his hair. Their feet ran lightly across his skin. Tom struggled to clear his vision. Insects flew at his nostrils. Tom blew violently through his nose. He could feel them in his ears...

Dropping to the ground, Tom crawled towards the magical pool and splashed water on his face. Burned by the spray, dead Stabiors fell like black rain around him.

Tom dipped his blade back into the pool and rolled away from the water's edge. Creta was nowhere to be seen.

"Look out, Tom!" Elenna screamed.

Tom whirled around, ducking instinctively. His sword hand flashed out – and the wet blade connected with something.

Creta's yellow eyes opened wide in shock. The monster was so close that Tom could see the serrated edges on the horns that lined its skull. Its jaws, open wide enough to take in the whole of Tom's head, fell slackly to its chest. Tom had stabbed the Beast right through the middle, where the swarm was.

The Beast roared and staggered as Tom yanked out his sword. Tom hoped desperately that it hadn't struck Captain Harkman. Hundreds of broken Stabiors scattered at his feet. Tom lashed out with his foot and pushed Creta hard.

The tottering Beast keeled over and fell into the pool. The Stabiors had no time to pull away from their host. There was a flash of white fire as Creta plunged into the water and disappeared. A great geyser erupted, shooting skywards. Tom and Elenna both heard an agonising shriek coming from deep beneath the pool's glittering surface. It was the voice of Malvel. Then the water settled to stillness.

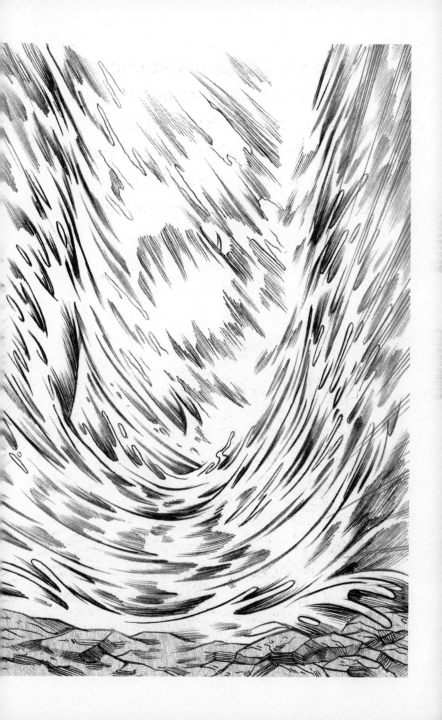

Tom held his breath. He hardly dared to hope that they had won! Creta and the ghastly Stabiors were no more. The water remained as still as glass – as if nothing had fallen in there at all.

"They've gone!" Elenna said. She stared up at where she had been fighting a swarm of bugs only moments before. Now there was nothing but the pure white fog drifting around her head. "Tom, you did it!"

Tom stepped back as something bubbled and exploded to the surface. His hand went to his sword. One more blow would do it, surely...

Coughing and spluttering, Captain Harkman floundered in the pool. His hair was plastered to his head. He was wearing the golden armour.

"I…" wheezed the captain. He kicked out feebly. Where the missing breastplate should have been, Tom could see his shirt had been ripped to shreds.

"We have to help him out of there!" Elenna said. "Before the weight of the armour drags him down…"

Elenna flung herself lengthways on the ground and stretched her hands out to where the captain was thrashing madly. Tom stretched out his arms as well. They both seized Captain Harkman's hands and dragged him out of the water.

The captain gazed around in bewilderment. "Where are we?" he asked, sounding dazed. "What was I doing in that pool?"

Tom grinned. "Having a swim, by the look of things," he joked.

Just then a flash burned away a slice of the deadening fog. Tom could see the sharp outline of the cliff, and the way the glittering river flowed down the gorge to fall away into the lost lakes of the Shadow Mountains.

"Well done! Oh, well done, Tom!"

came a familiar voice.

Aduro stood on the banks of the pool in a shimmering ring of fire. His arms were held wide, and he was smiling.

"What news of King Hugo's castle?" asked Elenna at once, moving towards Aduro. "And the Stabiors?"

"The plague is lifted and the creatures have gone," said Aduro. "Now, come. A great celebration awaits, and it cannot begin without you!"

The ring of fire where Aduro was standing rose and hovered above the magician. Tom, Elenna and Silver stepped forward to join him. After a moment's hesitation, so did Captain Harkman. Aduro waved his wand, and brought the ring of fire down around them all. The mists of the

Shadow Mountains faded, and so did
the shine of the magical waterfall.
Now all Tom could see was flames,
licking coolly about them. There was
a rush of wind. The flames vanished.

They were back in the throne-room
at the castle.

Happy faces met Tom and Elenna
everywhere they looked. Soldiers
and castle dwellers thronged around
them, saluting their captain, stroking
Silver, reaching out to them all and
welcoming them home. The drone of
the Stabiors had gone. Instead, the
air in the courtyard outside was filled
with the ringing sound of mallets
as the stonemasons set to work
repairing the damage.

Tom spun around, smiling and
clasping hands with the well-wishers,
exchanging glances with Elenna. But

where was Taladon? And how was Storm?

Taladon came forward, pushing through the crowd. His weathered face was set in a broad grin.

"Welcome home, son," Taladon said.

"Malvel has been defeated again!" Aduro called over the excited chatter of voices. "And it's all thanks to Tom and Elenna!"

"And Silver!" said Elenna, a little indignantly.

Laughter followed. Then the room fell into a respectful silence as King Hugo appeared. Tom bowed. Beside him, Elenna did the same.

"I thank you again," said the king warmly. "For driving this fresh peril from our kingdom. The skies are clear of Stabiors once more. And now

we know that the fabled water of the
Shadow Mountains exists after all."

"We would never have found it
without Marc's magic," said Tom,
smiling at Aduro's assistant. Marc
blushed with pleasure.

Everyone looked around as the Master-at-Arms came bustling into the throne room. His ferret lay snugly across his broad shoulders.

"The golden armour!" gasped the Master. "Look at the state of it!"

Tom looked down at his tarnished breastplate. Captain Harkman looked ashamed at the dents, smears and dirt on the armour that he was wearing.

"So much work!" said the Master.

Grinning, Marc lifted his wand and brought it down, and all at once, the armour was as pure, smooth and shining as ever.

"Hmm," said the Master. He reached fussily for the breastplate as Tom took it off. "Still a speck..." he muttered, and gave it a brisk rub with his sleeve. "There!"

Tom and Taladon walked out onto

the battlements. The air was golden and warm. Far on the horizon there was a flash and a gleam. Stonewin was erupting again.

"Now," Taladon remarked. "Where were we? A camping trip, I believe. It's time to pick up where we left off. The Western Shore for a bit of fishing, wasn't it? Are you ready?"

Tom looked down at the courtyard. Storm was being led out of his stable. His legs looked healed and strong. The stallion gazed up at the battlements and gave a whinny of joy when he recognised his master.

"I'm always ready," said Tom, with a smile.

JOIN TOM ON HIS NEXT
BEAST QUEST SOON!

Win an exclusive
Beast Quest T-shirt and goody bag!

In every Beast Quest book the Beast Quest logo is hidden
in one of the pictures. Find the logo in this book and
make a note of which page it appears on.
Send the page number in to us.
Each month we will draw one winner to receive
a Beast Quest T-shirt and goody bag.

Send your entry on a postcard listing
the title of this book and the winning
page number to:

THE BEAST QUEST COMPETITION:
CRETA THE WINGED TERROR
Orchard Books
338 Euston Road, London NW1 3BH
Australian readers should email:
childrens.books@hachette.com.au

New Zealand readers should write to:
Beast Quest Competition
4 Whetu Place, Mairangi Bay, Auckland, NZ
or email: childrensbooks@hachette.co.nz

Only one entry per child.
Final draw: 31 January 2011

You can also enter this competition
via the Beast Quest website: www.beastquest.co.uk

Join the Quest,
Join the Tribe

www.beastquest.co.uk

Have you checked out the all-new Beast Quest website?
It's the place to go for games, downloads, activities,
sneak previews and lots of fun!

You can read all about your favourite Beasts, download
free screensavers and desktop wallpapers for your
computer, and even challenge your friends
to a Beast Tournament.

Sign up to the newsletter at www.beastquest.co.uk
to receive exclusive extra content and the opportunity
to enter special members-only competitions. We'll send
you up-to-date info on all the Beast Quest books,
including the next exciting series which features
six brand-new Beasts!

Series 5: THE SHADE OF DEATH
OUT NOW!

Tom must travel to Gwildor, Avantia's twin kingdom, to free six new Beasts from an evil enchantment...

978 1 40830 437 2

978 1 40830 438 9

978 1 40830 439 6

978 1 40830 440 2

978 1 40830 441 9

978 1 40830 442 6

978 1 40830 436 5

Can Tom rescue the precious Cup of Life from a deadly two-headed demon?

Series 6: WORLD OF CHAOS
OUT MARCH 2010!

978 1 40830 723 6

978 1 40830 724 3

978 1 40830 725 0

978 1 40830 726 7

978 1 40830 727 4

978 1 40830 728 1

SPECIAL BUMPER EDITION!

Does Tom have the strength to triumph over cunning Creta?

978 1 40830 735 9

FROM THE DARK, A HERO ARISES...

Dare to enter the kingdom of Avantia.

A dark land, where wild creatures roam
and people fight tooth-and-nail to
survive another day.

And now, as the prophecies warned, a new evil
arises. Lord Derthsin – power-hungry and driven
by hatred – has ordered his armies into the
four corners of Avantia. Just one flicker
of hope remains...

If the four Beasts of Avantia can find their
Chosen Riders – and unite them into a deadly
fighting force – they might have the strength
to challenge Derthsin. But if they fail, the
land of Avantia will be lost forever...

OUT JULY 2010

www.thechroniclesofavantia.com